For_____

A Proud Ring Bearer

The
Ring Bearer

To Mike for teaching me that anything is possible — K. T.

To Noah and Emily for keeping my heart full of love,
my mind full of wonder and my clothes full of sticky goo — K. B.

To Vardan and Narek — N. D.

6th Avenue Books™ is an imprint of AOL Time Warner Book Group
An AOL Time Warner Company
1271 Avenue of the Americas
New York, NY 10020

Book designed by Paula Russell Szafranski

3   5   7   9   10   8   6   4   2

ISBN: 1-931722-39-0

Manufactured in China

The Ring Bearer

by Kathy Thomas and Kathleen Buckley

Illustrated by Norik Dilanchyan

Hi, my name is Matt, and I was the ring bearer in my Aunt Kim and Uncle Mike's wedding.

Aunt Kim told me it was an important job. But I didn't know what a ring bearer was. I thought I could dress up like a bear on Halloween.

Mom said I would carry the wedding rings down the aisle of the church on a pillow. I would wear a special suit called a tuxedo and walk with my cousin, Lori, who would be the flower girl.

I told Dad I was nervous about dropping the rings, so he gave me an old pillow for practice.

I practiced every day so I wouldn't drop the pillow.

I went to the store with
Grandpa to try on my
tuxedo. I got to wear
special shoes, too.
Grandpa said I would be
the best looking guy there.

The day before the wedding, Mom, Dad and I went to the rehearsal. I got to practice walking down the aisle with Lori. We didn't have to hold hands.

After the rehearsal, we all
went out to dinner. My aunt
and uncle thanked everyone
and gave us gifts.

The morning of the wedding, Mom helped me put on my tuxedo, and Dad helped me style my hair.

Mom gave me the real ring pillow for the wedding. I was nervous because I didn't want to lose the rings.

We arrived at the church, where I waited for my turn to walk down the aisle. There were lots of people watching, but I had to be brave.

I held my pillow straight and started walking to the front of the church.

Everyone smiled at me as I walked up next to Uncle Mike. I waited until the rings were needed, and then I held the pillow up high.

When the ceremony was over, everyone told me what a good job I did. Aunt Kim and Uncle Mike gave me big hugs and said they were proud of me.

After the ceremony, the photographer took lots of pictures. I had to stand still and smile.

The reception was really cool! I got to sit at a big people's table without Mom and Dad.

After dinner I ate a big piece
of wedding cake and danced
with Grandma and Lori.

When we got home, I went straight to bed. Aunt Kim let me keep the pillow, so I will remember the wedding for a long time. I'll remember how much fun I had being the ring bearer.